Ned Taylor

A Letter to Santa

igloobooks

It was Christmas Eve and Jenny and her little brother, James, were writing a letter to Santa.

Wriggling and giggling, they drew silly pictures and listed the presents they hoped that Santa would bring them.

Jenny put the letter into an envelope and left it near a glass of milk and a plate of cookies. "Santa will be sure to find it when he arrives," she said.

"Good idea," said James, sneakily munching on one of the cookies.

"I can't wait for Santa to get here," said James, as he and Jenny went upstairs to bed. Soon, all was quiet in the little house.

Downstairs, Mouse scurried out of his hole and onto the table. He began nibbling on a yummy cookie, when he spotted the letter.

"Someone's left an old envelope here," squeaked Mouse. "If I tear it up, it will make a warm, cosy blanket for my bed." He carried the envelope back to his hole and squished it through the doorway.

Later that night, there was a rumble and a bump.
Santa Claus had tumbled down the chimney with
his big sack of presents.

"Ho-ho-ho," said Santa, as he got to his feet.
He looked around the room for the letter from
Jenny and James, but he couldn't see it anywhere.
All he saw was a trail of cookie crumbs.

"That's strange," said Santa, following the trail to the mouse hole.

Santa peeped inside. There, he could see Mouse lying
in a bed made from old pencils and crayons. Beside it was a
set of matchbox drawers and a cotton-reel table. There were
even tiny Christmas decorations hanging all along the wall.

Mouse gave a long yawn. "Who's there?" he asked, sleepily. "Ho-ho-ho! It's Santa Claus!" said Santa, chuckling. "I'm looking for a very important letter from James and Jenny. Have you seen one?"

"Oh, no!" squeaked Mouse.
"I didn't know there was a letter
in the envelope, so I tore it up to
make a blanket. James and Jenny
will be really upset."

"Don't worry," said Santa. "You can
help me think of a present that they
would like instead." Mouse smiled
shyly and thought really hard.

"Well," said Mouse, "they both love to play outside in the snow. I think James would like a sledge to zoom down the snowy hills on. Jenny would love to whizz around the frozen lake on ice skates, too."

Santa reached into his sack.
"I have just the thing," he laughed.
He pulled out two golden presents and put them
under the tree. Mouse watched excitedly.
"I hope they like them," he squeaked.

"I think they'll love them," said Santa, waving goodbye. "There's a few special presents from me under the tree, too. Thanks for all your help, Mouse."

Mouse waved back at Santa until, with a whoosh, Santa disappeared back up the chimney.

Mouse yawned and stretched. He was very tired now and was ready to go back to sleep. He scampered back to his mouse hole and tucked himself back into bed.

Finally, Christmas morning came. Mouse was woken by squeals
of delight, as Jenny and James tore paper off their Christmas presents.
"Look, Jenny," said James. "There are two golden presents."

Jenny and James opened them excitedly. Jenny got a pair
of beautiful ice skates. "Wow! I've got a sledge!" said James.
"Let's go and play with them now."

James and Jenny wrapped up warm and ran outside into the bright, white snow. James whooshed down the hill on his sledge, climbed back to the top and whooshed down again.

"This is the best Christmas ever!" shouted Jenny, as she glided elegantly across the ice, spinning every so often.

Mouse was so happy that Jenny and James liked their presents. He was scuttling back to his hole when, out of the corner of his eye, he spotted a small present and an even smaller envelope under the tree.

When he got closer, Mouse saw that the letter had his name on.
"It's for me!" he squeaked.

Back in his hole, Mouse opened up the beautifully wrapped gift and found a warm, snuggly patchwork blanket inside. "Wow! This blanket looks so comfy," he said. Mouse opened the letter and read it aloud.

Dear Mouse,

Thank you for being so kind and helping me find presents for James and Jenny. One good turn deserves another, so here's a nice, comfy blanket to keep you warm all winter long.

Merry Christmas!
From
Santa

That night, Mouse snuggled underneath his new blanket and began to fall asleep.

He'd had so much fun helping Santa and choosing presents for Jenny and James. This was the best Christmas he'd ever had.